The GIRL
and the
DINOSAUR

For Sam, Nathan, and Charlotte —H. H.

For Eve —S. M.

BLOOMSBURY CHILDREN'S BOOKS
Bloomsbury Publishing Inc., part of Bloomsbury Publishing Plc
1385 Broadway, New York, NY 10018

BLOOMSBURY, BLOOMSBURY CHILDREN'S BOOKS, and the Diana logo
are trademarks of Bloomsbury Publishing Plc

First published in Great Britain in September 2019 by Bloomsbury Publishing Plc
Published in the United States of America in January 2020 by Bloomsbury Children's Books

Text copyright © 2019 by Hollie Hughes
Illustrations copyright © 2019 by Sarah Massini

Bloomsbury books may be purchased for business or promotional use. For information on bulk purchases please contact
Macmillan Corporate and Premium Sales Department at specialmarkets@macmillan.com

Library of Congress Cataloging-in-Publication Data
Names: Hughes, Hollie, author. | Massini, Sarah, illustrator.
Title: The girl and the dinosaur / by Hollie Hughes ; illustrated by Sarah Massini.
Description: New York : Bloomsbury, 2020.
Summary: Marianne has no friends until she unearths an entire dinosaur skeleton on the beach and
wishes that it would come to life.
Identifiers: LCCN 2019020794 (print) | LCCN 2019022138 (e-book)
ISBN 978-1-5476-0322-0 (hardcover) • ISBN 978-1-5476-0323-7 (e-book) • ISBN 978-1-5476-0324-4 (e-PDF)
Subjects: CYAC: Stories in rhyme. | Dinosaurs—Fiction. |
Friendship—Fiction. | Magic—Fiction.
Classification: LCC PZ8.3.H8664 Gir 2020 (print) | LCC PZ8.3.H8664 (e-book) | DDC [E]—dc23
LC record available at https://lccn.loc.gov/2019020794

Art created with watercolor, pencil, printed pattern collage, and Photoshop
Typeset in Landa
Book design and hand lettering by Kristina Coates
Printed in China by C&C Offset Printing Co., Ltd., Shenzhen, Guangdong
2 4 6 8 10 9 7 5 3 1

All papers used by Bloomsbury Publishing Plc are natural, recyclable products made from wood grown in well-managed forests.
The manufacturing processes conform to the environmental regulations of the country of origin.

To find out more about our authors and books visit www.bloomsbury.com and sign up for our newsletters.

The GIRL and the DINOSAUR

Hollie Hughes

illustrated by

Sarah Massini

BLOOMSBURY
CHILDREN'S BOOKS
NEW YORK LONDON OXFORD NEW DELHI SYDNEY

There's a town beside the sea,
not so very far from here,
with golden sands and rock pools
and a tattered, battered pier.

And there's a girl upon the beach—
her name is Marianne;
she's digging for a dinosaur
just beneath the sand.

Now, the fisherfolk all worry
for the girl beside the sea.
"She needs to find some *friends*," they say,
"and let those *old bones* be."

Still, Marianne is patient,
and Marianne is clever,

and **stony bone**
by **stony bone** . . .

...a *beastie* comes together.

"I think I'll name you **Bony**," whispers little Marianne. "And now that we are friends, I'll be the **best** one that I can."

But the sleepy sun is setting,
and Marianne must go.
"Sleep tight," she says to Bony,
"I'll be back before you know."

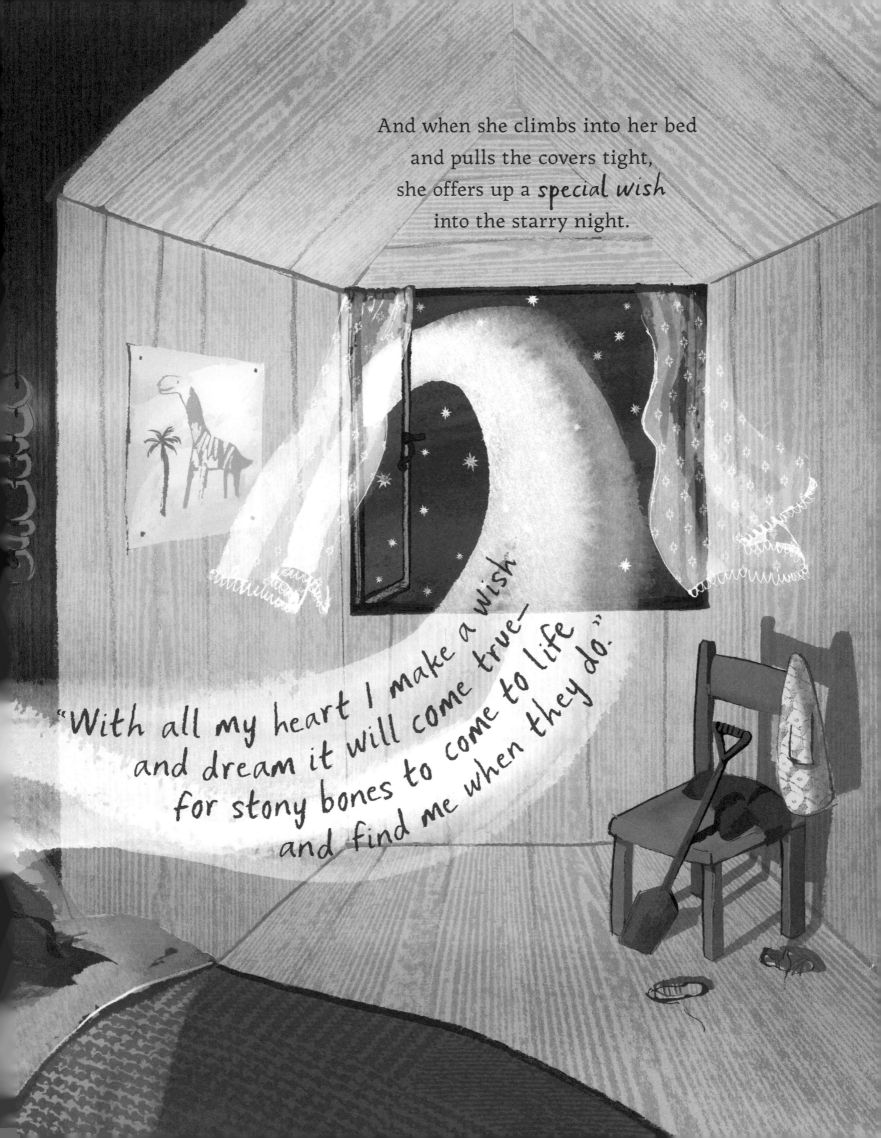

And when she climbs into her bed
and pulls the covers tight,
she offers up a **special** *wish*
into the starry night.

"With all my heart I make a wish
and dream it will come true—
for stony bones to come to life
and find me when they do."

The wishing stars burn **bright** that night,
the air is thick with *dreams*,

and a deeply sleeping dinosaur
is waking up, it seems . . .

Then a *tap-tap* at the window—
and Marianne's awake!
Her wishes have come **true**,
and there are memories to make.

A bendy neck is offered
for a girl to slide right down,
and magic is now promised
in the sleepy, starlit town.

Happily together, the friends go to the sea,
to bob with boats and fishes, their spirits wild and free.

Then on to new adventures
up a winding path of trees,
and they're flashing through a forest
like leaves upon the breeze.

Fairies float beside them
on their way to who knows what—
past *unicorns* and *giants*
and creatures long forgot.

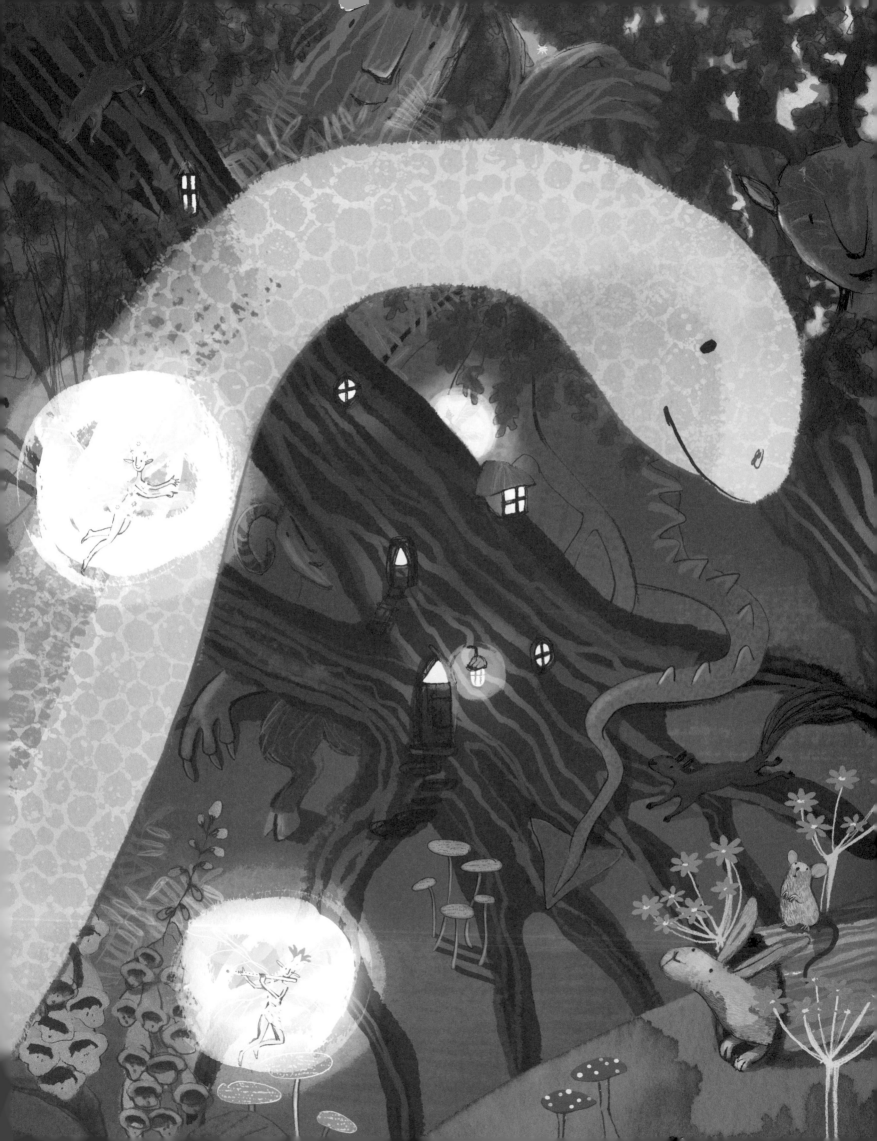

Up they climb, still higher,
hearts beating *boom-boom* fast,
till they reach a mountain summit
and stop for breath at last.

And as the clouds all part,
they spy a land up in the sky—
a *magical* moonlit island
where night and daydreams fly.

With a mighty leap of faith, our brave dinosaur takes flight,
and then the pair are soaring through the dreamscape of the night.

Swooping,
gliding,
flying...

to the land up in the air . . .

And—*oh!*—what fun and magic
awaits the two friends there!

A **party** place for children and
the creatures from their dreams,
where *anything* is possible
and *nothing's* as it seems.

But slumber's pull is beckoning the children back to town . . .

It's time to leave the island
and begin the journey down.

Back to the town beside the sea,
and back to empty beds,
and back to secret memories
to keep from grown-up heads.

And when Marianne snuggles down
and pulls her covers *tight*,
she slips into a dream-filled sleep
of *magic* in the night.

So, there's a town beside the sea,
not very far from here,
with golden sands and rock pools
and a tattered, battered pier.

And there are children on the beach
with little Marianne,
each digging for their dinosaur
just beneath the sand.

The fisherfolk are happy now,
and everything is well . . .

And as for **magic** in the night,
the children will not tell.